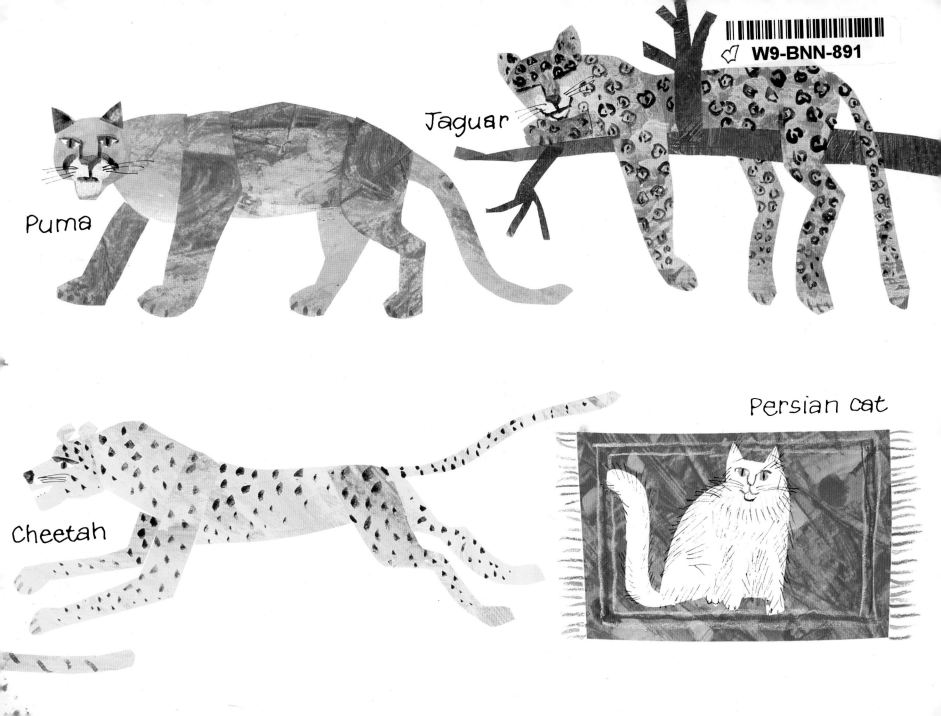

Puma

Jaguar

W9-BNN-891

Cheetah

Persian cat

Dedicated to all the cats in my life

Eric Carle Have you seen my cat?

Simon & Schuster Books for Young Readers

Have you seen my cat?

Have you seen my cat?

Have you seen
my cat?

This is not <u>my</u> cat!

This is not <u>my</u> cat!

This is not <u>my</u> cat!

Have you seen my cat?

This is not my cat!

Have you seen my cat?

This is not <u>my</u> cat!

Have you seen my cat?

This is not <u>my</u> cat!

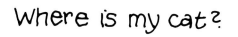

where is my cat?

Have you seen my cat?

Simon and Schuster Books for Young readers.
An imprint of Simon & Schuster
Children's Publishing Division
1230 Avenue of the Americas
New York, NY 10020
Also available in a Simon & Schuster Books for Young Readers edition.
Printed and bound in the United States of America
20 19 18 17 16 15 14 13 12

The Library of Congress has cataloged the hardcover edition as follows:
Carle, Eric.
Have you seen my cat?
Originally published: New York: F. Watts, 1973.
Summary: A young boy encounters all sorts of cats while searching for the one he
lost.
(1. Cats—Fiction. 2. Picture books) I. Title.
PZ7.C21476Hav   1987   [E]   87-15262
ISBN 0-88708-054-5
ISBN 0-689-81731-2 (Aladdin pbk.)

Ask your bookseller for these other **Simon & Schuster Books for Young Readers** titles by Eric Carle:
All Around Us
A House For Hermit Crab
The Greedy Python/The Foolish Tortoise, by Richard Buckley
The Mountain that Loved a Bird, by Alice McLerran
Pancakes, Pancakes
Papa, Please Get the Moon for Me
Rooster's Off to See the World
The Tiny Seed

Lion

Bobcat

Panther

Tiger